The Tooth Fairy Meets El Ratón Pérez

by René Colato Laínez

illustrated by Tom Lintern

TRICYCLE PRESS
Berkeley

Miguelito wiggled and jiggled his loose tooth until one night, it fell out.

"Yay! *Mi diente,* my tooth," he said, and put it under his pillow.

Soon Miguelito fell asleep.

Far away in her castle, the Tooth Fairy read
fan letters,
counted coins,
and searched for addresses.
When she saw a star begin to twinkle in the sky,
she rushed for her magic wand.
"Fantastic! The signal!" she said. "A new tooth!"

Meanwhile, in his cave, El Ratón Pérez rolled
out his maps,
practiced his lasso,
and worked on his rocket ship.
He looked at the moon and licked his whiskers.
Then he saw the moonbeam.
"Finally, the signal!" he said. "A new *diente*."

Tap…tap…tap—clap! "Here is my tooth!"

Creep…creep…creep—leap! "¡Aquí está, mi diente!"

"Eeeeek, a mouse!"

"*¡Guau, una señorita bonita!*"

"Who are you?" the Tooth Fairy asked.

"I am El Ratón Pérez," he said, bowing. "I collect lost teeth from *niños* around the world."

The Tooth Fairy smiled, shaking her wand. "I am the Tooth Fairy, and here in the United States, I collect children's teeth." She tugged at the tooth.

"No, no, no," said El Ratón Pérez, tugging back. "This is Miguelito's house, and I collected his *papá's*, *mamá's*, and his *abuelitos'* teeth. Miguelito's tooth is mine."

The Tooth Fairy grabbed the tooth from one
side. El Ratón Pérez grabbed it from the other.
They pulled and pushed, and pushed and pulled.

"It's mine!"

"¡Es mío!"

"Stop shoving your whiskers in my face!"
"Don't poke my nose with that funny stick!"
Whoosh! The tooth flew through the air.
"Oh no! The tooth!"
"*¡Ay caramba! ¡El diente!*"

The Tooth Fairy flew to the closet. "Where is my tooth?" She hopped from hanger to hanger, lighting the way with her magic wand.

El Ratón Pérez rushed to the floor below the
dresser. He searched, sniffing from shoe to shoe.
"*¿Dónde está mi diente?*"

Suddenly, they saw something sparkling high on a bookshelf.

El Ratón Pérez jumped and pointed. "*Mi diente* is up there! I will get it."

He launched his lasso at the shelf, but the rope was too short. He tried again and again, but it was no use.

"*¡Ay caramba!* I cannot reach *mi diente*," El Ratón Pérez said.

"The tooth will be mine," cheered the Tooth Fairy.

She flew to the shelf and tried to push the books aside, but the books were too heavy.

"The space is too narrow for me. I will never reach my tooth," she said, flying back down to sit next to El Ratón Pérez.

"It is a beautiful tooth!" the Tooth Fairy said with tears rolling down her face.

"*Es un bello diente*," El Ratón Pérez agreed with tears in his whiskers. "I can squeeze into small places, but I cannot crawl up that high."

"Wait a minute," the Tooth Fairy said. "Let's rescue our tooth together! I'll carry you up."

"*Sí!*" he said. "Then I'll crawl between the books."

El Ratón Pérez carefully perched on the Tooth Fairy's shoulder.

"Hold on!" she cried.

They flew up to the shelf together.

"I see our *diente*!" said El Ratón Pérez.

He helped the Tooth Fairy push aside the books,
then squeezed in and triumphantly pulled out the tooth.
"Hooray!" said the Tooth Fairy.
"*Sí. ¡Viva! ¡Viva!*" cheered El Ratón Pérez.

"Let's share *el diente*," said El Ratón Pérez.
"I am using *mis dientes* to build a rocket ship
so I can visit the moon made of cheese. You
can come with me!"

"And after our trip, I can use the teeth from
the rocket ship to build a sparkling castle!" said
the Tooth Fairy.

"Yes!" they shouted, dancing around the tooth.

The following morning, Miguelito found two shiny coins under his pillow with a note that said:

From your amigos
forever,
the Tooth Fairy
and El Ratón Pérez

Author's Note

Since the Middle Ages, the Tooth Fairy and El Ratón Pérez have been part of oral traditions around the world. In the United States and English-speaking countries, the Tooth Fairy collects lost teeth from children. In Latin America and most European countries, children put their teeth under their pillow for a little mouse instead of the Tooth Fairy. In France she is called *La Petite Souris*. In Italy his name is *Topino*. In Spain and Latin America his name is *El Ratón Pérez*. Both the Tooth Fairy and El Ratón Pérez always leave a special gift in return for a shiny, healthy tooth!

Who are the Tooth Fairy and El Ratón Pérez?

Name: The Tooth Fairy

Birthplace: England

What does she do with the teeth? She uses them to make sparkling castles.

Legend: The Tooth Fairy keeps the teeth she collects away from witches and bad spirits who want the teeth to prepare evil potions!

Name: El Ratón Pérez

Birthplace: Spain (first appearing in a book in 1894, when Luis Colma wrote the story for a young King Alfonso XIII)

What does he do with the teeth? He uses them to build a rocket ship to go to the moon.

Legend: In exchange for taking their teeth, El Ratón Pérez promises children that their new teeth will grow in just as straight and healthy as his own.

Spanish Terms in This Book

Mi diente/Mis dientes: My tooth/My teeth.

Aquí está: Here it is.

¡Guau!: Wow!

Señorita bonita: Beautiful young lady.

Niños: Children.

Papá: Father.

Mamá: Mother.

Abuelitos: Grandparents.

Es mío: It is mine.

¡Ay caramba!: Oh no!

¿Dónde está?: Where is it?

Bello: Beautiful.

Sí: Yes.

¡Viva! ¡Viva!: Hooray!

Amigos: Friends.

To my nephews and nieces and their lost dientes
that now are part of a rocket ship. —R.C.L.

To my niece and nephew, Ava and Gavin. —T.L.

Published in the United States by Tricycle Press, an imprint of the Crown Publishing Group,
a division of Random House, Inc., New York.
www.crownpublishing.com
www.triclepress.com

Tricycle Press and the Tricycle Press colophon are registered trademarks of Random House, Inc.

Library of Congress Cataloging-in-Publication Data

Colato Laínez, René.
The Tooth Fairy meets El Ratón Pérez / by René Colato Laínez ;
illustrations by Tom Lintern. — 1st ed.
p. cm.
Summary: When Miguel loses a tooth, two legendary characters come to claim
it—one who is responsible for collecting teeth in the United States and one
who has collected the teeth of the boy's parents and grandparents.
[1. Tooth Fairy—Fiction. 2. Teeth—Fiction. 3. Hispanic
Americans—Fiction.] I. Lintern, Tom, ill. II. Title.
PZ7.C66995Too 2010
[E]—dc22
2009016782

ISBN 978-1-58246-296-7 (hardcover)
ISBN 978-1-58246-342-1 (Gibraltar lib. bdg.)

Printed in China

Design by Christy Hale

Typeset in Minion Pro
The illustrations in this book were rendered in pencil then edited using Photoshop.

1 2 3 4 5 6 — 15 14 13 12 11 10

First Edition